CHARLES DICKENS

by L. DU GARDE PEACH,
M.A., Ph.D., D.Litt.

with illustrations by
JOHN KENNEY

Publishers: Wills & Hepworth Ltd., Loughborough

First published 1965   ©   *Printed in England*

CHARLES DICKENS

Charles Dickens, one of the greatest story-tellers in the English or any other language, was born in Portsea in 1812. His father was a clerk in the Navy Pay Office, and had very little money. When young Charles was only two years old the family moved to Chatham, and it was here that he lived until he was nine.

Chatham was a wonderful place for a young boy. Later, in one of his books, he described his surroundings as consisting of "soldiers, sailors, Jews, chalk, shrimps, offices, and dock-yard men."

All round Chatham in those days, long before motor cars or even railways, was the beautiful country of the chalk hills and valleys, the deep lanes and the marshes. All of these things were retained in Charles' memory, to be used later in his books.

In one of his greatest books, 'David Copper-field', Dickens tells how little David, on his long, lonely walk from London to Dover, slept one night in a grass-grown battery overhanging a lane, lying down beside an old cannon, com-forted by the footsteps of a sentry who had no idea he was there. Charles had no doubt climbed on just such a cannon in his days in Chatham.

When Charles Dickens was nine the family moved to London, and the happy days of wandering over the chalk downs, or exploring the waterfront, were over. Instead, John Dickens took his wife and family to live in a dingy London street, where very soon he got into debt.

In those days people who could not pay their debts were sent to a very unpleasant prison called the Marshalsea. Here Mr. Dickens soon found himself, leaving his wife and family to fend for themselves as best they could.

Mrs. Dickens was desperately poor and it was necessary that Charles should earn some money. So at the age of ten he was sent to work in a factory where blacking was made, and day after day he sat in a dingy cellar pasting labels on pots of blacking. For this he was paid six shillings a week.

The visits which Charles paid to his father in the Marshalsea, and the unhappy time he spent in the blacking factory, were all remembered when he came to write 'David Copperfield'. David is described as working in a warehouse with decaying floors and staircase, where old grey rats scuffled down in the cellar.

Dickens drew a picture somewhat like his father in the character of Mr. Micawber in 'David Copperfield'. Mr. Micawber, whose picture you can see opposite, was also very poor, and was always waiting for something to turn up. Something turned up for Mr. Dickens. He inherited a little money and was able to leave the Marshalsea prison.

Charles was also able to leave the blacking factory. For two or three years he went back to school, and if the boys' schools which he later described in his books were anything like those of his own schooldays, he could not have been very happy.

His schooling did not last very long, and when he was only fourteen or fifteen he was taken into the office of a solicitor in the famous Gray's Inn in London.

Nothing that came his way was ever forgotten by Charles Dickens. The year and a half which he spent in the solicitor's office provided him with many memories of the queer people he met, as well as with enough knowledge of the law itself to enable him, in after years, to write some wonderfully amusing tales of the law and lawyers. Already he was gathering his material.

Dickens had no intention of remaining a lawyer's clerk. With the object of getting a better position, he set himself to learn shorthand, in those days a more difficult matter than it is to-day.

Soon he was expert enough to become a newspaper reporter on the 'Morning Chronicle'. As such he had often to make journeys to places distant from London. These journeys were made along bad roads in horse-drawn coaches. In later years he wrote:

"I have often transcribed for the printer from my shorthand notes important public speeches, writing on the palm of my hand, by the light of a dark lantern, in a post-chaise and four, galloping through a wild country and through the dead of night, at the then surprising rate of fifteen miles an hour."

Another picture of the conditions in which he worked was later described by him: "I do verily believe I have been upset in every description of vehicle; I have been belated on miry roads, towards the small hours, fifty miles from London, in a wheel-less carriage, with exhausted horses, and have got back in time for publication." Such memories he later made use of in his stories again and again.

Charles Dickens had been writing stories ever since he was a boy at school. Now, like all people who write stories, he wanted to see one of them in print. So at the age of twenty-one he carefully wrote out a fair copy of a story called 'A Dinner at Poplar Walk'.

There was in London a publication called the Monthly Magazine, and young Mr. Dickens, greatly daring, decided to send his story to the editor. To save postage he went to the offices of the magazine and dropped it into the letter box.

It was not a very good story, but it was published, and Dickens afterwards wrote that when he saw it actually in print, his eyes dimmed with tears of joy and pride. It was a great day for Charles Dickens, but an even greater day if they had only known it, for millions of people all over the world.

You can read this story for yourself in a book called 'Sketches by Boz'. The title has been changed to 'Mr. Minns and his Cousin'. Charles was not paid anything for his story: perhaps he did not expect to be. His happiness at seeing it in print was all the reward he wanted.

Dickens was a natural born story-teller, never happier than when he was writing. Now that he had found someone to publish his stories he was happier still. Although he afterwards became a very good business man, at twenty-one he was too young, or perhaps too happy, to worry about whether he was paid or not. All he wanted to do was to write.

Soon there were enough stories to make a book, and they were published in two volumes. The name 'Boz', with which Dickens signed them, was the nick-name of his favourite brother when he was a boy. It was to become one of the most famous nick-names in the world.

Dickens was paid at last. For the book of sketches he got a hundred and fifty guineas, a great sum in those days, and a fortune for a young writer.

The success of 'Sketches by Boz' brought more than money to young Mr. Dickens: it brought a visit from two important gentlemen. They were Messrs. Chapman and Hall, publishers. They had come to invite 'Boz', whom they now found to their surprise to be a young man of twenty-four, to write numerous descriptions for some sporting drawings.

Dickens knew nothing about sport. Hunting, shooting, fishing, even cricket, were beyond him. As a young man he was anxious to earn money, but as an author he refused to write about things of which he knew nothing.

Chapman and Hall had suggested a club of sportsmen, and the drawings were to be of their misfortunes. Dickens suggested that the adventures of this group of men should consist of other things besides sporting mishaps, and finally Chapman and Hall agreed. The subjects were to be left to the author.

The name of Mr. Pickwick is to-day known to everyone, and our picture shows what he and Sam Weller looked like. In fact the name of Mr. Pickwick fits him so well that it is difficult to imagine that Dickens thought of all sorts of names before he decided on Pickwick.

The Pickwick Papers came out in monthly parts. Of the first number only four hundred were sold, but by the time the fifteenth came out, the number had risen to forty thousand. Everybody wanted to read about Mr. Pickwick's latest adventures, and as the coaches brought the new numbers from London to other towns, crowds waited to buy copies wherever the coach stopped.

In his twenty-fifth year Charles Dickens had suddenly become one of the best known writers in the country. From being poor, he had by his own efforts suddenly become rich, and because of this he was able to marry the daughter of his first publisher.

If we could go back in time and see the wedding of Charles Dickens and Catherine Hogarth, we should see an England very different from the one we know to-day. They were married on an April day in 1836, just over a year before Queen Victoria came to the throne.

The railways were only just beginning to carry passengers and were very slow and uncomfortable. Most travelling was still done in horse-drawn coaches. The roads were rough, and a speed of more than eight or ten miles an hour was considered fast.

The clothes worn by both men and women look very unpractical to us. They certainly wore far more clothes than people do to-day. The picture on the opposite page shows you how our ancestors dressed in 1836. The long dresses of the women must have got very dirty because the streets of the towns were often deep in mud.

We must remember that Charles Dickens was a very practical man. He liked to *do* things, as well as write about them. Also, all his life he was full of energy and hated ever to be idle.

He was always ready to do two or three things at once, and whilst still writing 'Pickwick', Dickens became the editor of a new magazine called 'Bentley's Miscellany', in which the novel 'Oliver Twist' appeared. He was now writing two great novels and editing a magazine at the same time.

Even this was not enough to satisfy his energetic nature. He would often go down into the printing works and watch the compositors setting the type.

In those days all books and newspapers were set by hand. That is, the letters were all separate pieces of metal, and were taken one after another out of the compartments of a wooden type-case to make words and sentences. The men who did this became very clever at picking up each letter from the right compartment without looking at it. When they had set a page, it was locked in an iron frame called a 'chase'. We may be sure that Charles Dickens tried his hand at it.

'Oliver Twist' was a story written with a purpose. Already in 'Pickwick', Dickens had made people ashamed of the terrible Marshalsea prison, and it is partly due to him that such prisons no longer exist. In 'Oliver Twist' he was to make people realise how the poor were treated by some of the people paid to look after them.

Dickens had been very poor when he was a boy. All his life he tried in his stories to shame people into doing away with cruelty to those less fortunate than themselves. He did this very cleverly because his stories were so good that everybody read them.

In 'Oliver Twist' there is a character called Bumble. He is the Beadle, the man who used to carry out the orders of a sort of parish council. In the character of Bumble, Dickens has shown what happened to poor orphans like Oliver Twist when a big, bullying man, full of his own importance, and with no sympathy, was in charge of them. This was all very real in Dickens' day.

Poor little hungry Oliver once asked for more gruel. You must read the book one day and find out what happened to him.

Charles Dickens was a very good actor. He used to take part in plays arranged privately by his friends, and before he had begun to write 'Pickwick' he had tried his hand at writing plays.

They were not very good plays, though one of them, called 'The Great Winglebury Duel', ran for seventy nights in London. He also wrote an operetta, but everybody said it was so bad that he never wrote another.

In Dickens' time the plays which people went to see were either what were called melodramas, very dramatic plays, or humorous farces. Dickens could write very funny books like 'The Pickwick Papers', but somehow his kind of fun was not suited to the stage.

Dickens has described some of the theatres of his day very unkindly. Many of them were certainly very rough, with noisy, unruly audiences. According to Dickens they were owned by the lowest sort of characters. Even the best theatres in London were a great deal noisier and rougher than the theatres of to-day. If the audience disliked the play they threw orange peel and even bottles at the actors. This was unfair. They ought to have thrown them at the author, but he was not there.

Most children to-day enjoy going to school, but when Dickens was a boy, children used to dread school and were very unhappy when the holidays came to an end.

In his next story, 'Nicholas Nickleby', Dickens' intention was to let everybody know what some of these schools were like. The school in the book is called Dotheboys Hall, and Dickens tells us that it is only a faint and feeble picture of schools which really existed: they must have been very unpleasant places indeed.

Nicholas Nickleby went to the school as an assistant master. This is what it looked like when he got there: "a bare and dirty room with a couple of windows, whereof a tenth part might be glass, the remainder being stopped up with old copybooks and paper. There were a couple of long, old, rickety desks, cut and notched and inked and damaged in every possible way."

Mr. Squeers was the headmaster of the school, and a very unpleasant man he was. His wife, who was worse, used to dose the unfortunate pupils with a horrible mixture of treacle and brimstone every day before breakfast.

As a boy, Dickens had grown up in the atmosphere of the docks and ships of Chatham, and all his life he loved the sea. As he grew older and could live where he liked, much of his time was spent in Brighton or Dover or Broadstairs. The last of these, then a quiet little fishing village on the far east coast of Kent, was his favourite.

The house in which he lived in Broadstairs came to be known as Bleak House, the name of a novel which he wrote after his last visit.

It would be difficult to recognise the Broadstairs of to-day from his description of it about 1840. In a letter he describes both it and himself. "This is a little fishing place, intensely quiet, built on a cliff, whereon our house stands. In a bay window, from nine o'clock to one, sits a gentleman with rather long hair and no neckcloth, who writes and grins, as if he thought he were very funny indeed. His name is Boz."

A seaside bathing beach in 1840 looked like the picture on the opposite page, with its queer bathing machines and the quite unsuitable clothes of the men and women.

To-day we are used to having holidays at the seaside or in the country. In the first half of last century, when Dickens lived, most people in England could not afford holidays. Places like Blackpool and Southend and Margate were small villages, and even if people wished to go there, the journey was slow and difficult.

As for going for a holiday on the continent, that was only possible for rich people who had the time and the money. The motor coaches and private cars of to-day were undreamed of even a hundred years ago.

Most people stayed at home, because for one thing there were no such privileges as holidays with pay, and for another, the workers in the factories only had a few days off.

They made their holidays bright in their own way, and in their own little towns and villages. It was a poor sort of village which did not have its sports and festivals. We find descriptions of these in Dickens' books. He loved to see people enjoying themselves, and he was always ready to join in and enjoy himself with them. That is one of the reasons why Dickens' stories were so popular with everybody.

Dickens has left us wonderful pictures of the way people lived their ordinary everyday lives in the first half of last century. A description by him of the changing of the horses of a stage-coach, at an inn, is almost as good as if we could see a film of it. This was something which was happening all over Britain hundreds of times every day and night, but only Dickens thought of describing it.

"Four horses with cloths on—change for a coach—were standing quietly at the corner of the yard, surrounded by a listless group of post-boys in shiny hats and smock frocks. A few loungers were collected round the horse-trough, awaiting the arrival of the coach.

"Suddenly the loud notes of a bugle break the monotonous stillness of the street. In comes the coach, rattling over the uneven paving. Down get the outsides, out come the waiters, up start the hostlers, and the loungers, and the post-boys, as if they were electrified—unstrapping, and unchaining, and unbuckling, and dragging willing horses out, and forcing reluctant horses in.

"Up get the outsides again, and the guard, and the coachmen. 'All right!' is the cry, and away they go."

Charles Dickens was interested in any kind of show, from performing dogs to Punch and Judy. This was because he was a very good actor himself, and had taken part in many amateur performances.

He was not always kind to the little travelling companies of actors which he described. He saw very clearly what was funny or peculiar about them and exaggerated it.

In 'Nicholas Nickleby' you can read a very amusing account of the company which the young hero of the book joined, and of Mr. and Mrs. Crummles and the other actors. He first met Mr. Crummles at an inn, and when he entered the room a very strange sight met his eyes. This is how Dickens describes it.

"At the upper end of the room were a couple of boys, one of them very tall, and the other very short, both dressed as sailors, fighting what is called in the playbills, a terrific combat. The short boy had gained a great advantage over the tall boy, who was reduced to mortal strait, and both were overlooked by a large, heavy man, perched on the corner of a table." This was Mr. Crummles himself, the manager of the company.

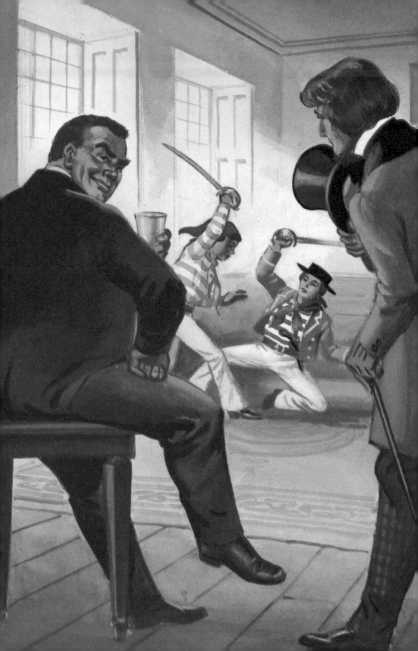

Dickens wrote most of his stories about the queer people whom he met or invented, like Mr. Pickwick or Mr. Micawber. In addition to these he wrote two novels about historical people and events.

These two books were about exciting happenings of which we can read in history books. Dickens wrote a history book himself, called 'A Child's History of England', and he knew all about the French Revolution and the riots in London which were the historical background of his stories.

History is made by people. Not only the kings and generals, the chancellors and archbishops whom we learn about at school, but by ordinary people living ordinary lives. It is when these ordinary lives are all upset by revolutions or wars that they become interesting to a writer like Dickens.

Not only did he make interesting stories about his imaginary characters, but he made the real characters and the events of history seem more real to us. We feel as we read, that we are taking part in these exciting events of so long ago. The French Revolution in 1789 was a terrible time for the people of France. Our picture shows something of what it was like.

When he was thirty years old Dickens went to America, crossing the Atlantic in winter in a ship which still had sails, but also great paddle-wheels to help it along when the wind failed. His account of a storm at sea shows how vividly he could describe anything which had happened to him.

Dickens did not like America, and the Americans did not like him because of the things he wrote about them. Fortunately, on his next visit, he liked them much better, and he became very popular.

One of the reasons for Dickens' dislike of America was that his books were being printed and sold there without any payment to him. This was because in those days there was no arrangement between countries for paying foreign authors. This has now been altered.

We have seen that Dickens went about with his eyes very wide open. He made use of everything that he saw, and it is not surprising that on his return to England he wrote another novel, 'Martin Chuzzlewit', in which some part of the story takes place in America. The Americans did not like this either, probably because a lot of what he wrote was much too near the truth.

Like most other people, Dickens loved Christmas. Over and over again in his books he has written of happy Christmas parties like the one in our picture.

The most famous is the short story of 'A Christmas Carol'. Everybody knows the old miser Scrooge, and how his heart was softened at Christmas time by the three Spirits, and how he sent the very biggest turkey to the home of Tiny Tim. It is not one of Dickens' best stories, but it is one of his happiest. It is also one which in after years he enjoyed reading to an audience. This was because it contained much from his own life.

'A Christmas Carol' is a story to read at Christmas. Many people read it *every* Christmas. But it is not the only story in which Dickens writes about the happiest time of the year. One of the early 'Sketches by Boz' is called 'A Christmas Dinner'. This is how Dickens describes it:

"A Christmas party! We know nothing in nature more delightful! There seems a magic in the very name of Christmas. Kindly hearts are united, and all is kindness and benevolence. Would that Christmas lasted the whole year round."

Dickens spent many long hours writing at his desk, looking like the picture opposite, but when he wrote his best known book, 'David Copperfield', he was a clean-shaven young man.

This novel is what we call autobiographical, which is a very long word meaning that the author is writing about himself. David Copperfield is Charles Dickens. We may be sure that what little David thinks in the book, is very much what young Charles Dickens thought as a boy in London.

The blacking warehouse, the poor district in London, the Marshalsea prison, the hard work, and even his likeable but unsuccessful father— all these appear in the story of 'David Copperfield'.

We can still see the opening pages of 'David Copperfield', just as Dickens wrote them, in the South Kensington Museum, in London. It is interesting to find that he tried all sorts of names for the hero. He has written Copperboy, Copperstone, and Copperfull, before he decided on Copperfield. There are also many corrections in different coloured inks. We can almost see Dickens remembering his own boyhood days, and altering or adding as the memories came into his mind. This is one reason why the story is so real.

During all these years whilst he was becoming more and more famous, Dickens had lived in many places in various countries. He had had houses in France and Italy, as well as in London and on the south coast of England. Now, as one of the best known writers in the world, and with plenty of money, he bought the house in which he was to live for the rest of his life.

He also at the same time made a dream of little Charles Dickens come true. As a small boy he had looked at a rather peculiar house at Gad's Hill, near Chatham, and thought how wonderful it would be to live in a house like that. His father had once said to him that if he were to work hard, he might one day have it for his own.

John Dickens little thought that his words to his little son Charles would come true. That is exactly what happened. Because forty years later Dickens bought Gad's Hill.

In 1858 he wrote to a friend: "My little place is a grave, red-brick house, which I have added to and stuck bits upon in all manner of ways."

Dickens enjoyed reading his own stories aloud. He was persuaded to do so before a paying audience to raise money to help the family of an old friend. It was then that the idea came to him of giving public readings for his own benefit.

For the last ten years of his life these public readings became famous in England and America. Dickens had always been a good actor, and now he was able to act all the odd people his imagination had created. He made them so real that even he himself is said to have wept over some of the affecting scenes in his books.

An entertainment of this sort was something very new in 1860. Dickens had no scenery or special costume. He used to appear on a bare platform with a small reading desk. The characters were all made real to the audience by the wonderful way in which he acted them.

It was the travelling from place to place in all sorts of weather and by all sorts of conveyances, which was in the end too much for his strength. However ill he felt, and in America he became very ill indeed, he would never disappoint an audience.

It was during one of these journeys that a railway accident happened in which Dickens was involved. He was injured, but many passengers were killed or seriously hurt. Dickens worked alongside the rescuers for many hours.

The shock to his nerves was great and he never really recovered from it. He was still suffering from the effects when he went to America on a tour of lectures and public readings.

Railway accidents are always terrible. They were probably no more frequent in Dickens' time than they are to-day, but the railways in 1864 were less efficient, and nurses and doctors and ambulances could not be rushed to the scene of an accident as they are now.

The trains of 1864 would look very strange to us, and soon, when steam engines have disappeared entirely from our railways, they will seem stranger still. The coaches also were very different from the comfortable corridor coaches' we know. Our picture shows the kind of train on which Dickens travelled, and the accident which happened to it near Staplehurst in Kent. Although the train was not travelling as fast as do the diesel trains, the coaches were not as strongly built as those of to-day.

Dickens was working on his last book, 'The Mystery of Edwin Drood', when he died at his home at Gad's Hill. We do not know how Dickens meant the story to end, nor do we know the solution of the mystery. Many authors have tried to finish the book, but none successfully.

This is because there has never been another English author who could write quite like Dickens. He had a way of telling a story as though he himself were enjoying every minute of it. And because he enjoyed it, so do we.

This is also the reason why so many of his characters are so well known to people who have never read any of his books. Little Oliver Twist asking for more, Mr. Micawber waiting for something to turn up, Uriah Heep who was so 'umble, and Tiny Tim who did NOT die— these and many others have become part of the English language. No other writer except Shakespeare has invented so many characters which are still constantly referred to, and phrases which are still in use.

At the end of his eager, busy life, only three months before he died, Dickens achieved the supreme honour of being received by Queen Victoria at Buckingham Palace.

Mr. Turveydrop
'Bleak House'

Dolly Varden
'Barnaby Rudge'

Mr. Pecksniff
'Martin Chuzzlewit'

Newman Noggs
'Nicholas Nickleby'

Mr. Squeers
'Nicholas Nickleby'

Fanny Squeers
'Nicholas Nickleby'

Scrooge
'A Christmas Carol'

Mr. Dick
'David Copperfield'

Uriah Heep
'David Copperfield'